BUILD YOUR OWN ADVENTURE

CONTENTS

Meet Harry

Harry Potter is a young wizard who attends the magical Hogwarts School of Witchcraft and Wizardry. Harry is good-hearted and very brave. He has lots of exciting magical adventures. Harry never goes looking for trouble, but trouble often finds him!

Muggle life

Until he was eleven years old, Harry lived with his aunt and uncle on a street called Privet Drive. They didn't have magical powers and tried to stop Harry finding out that magic existed. Witches and wizards call non-magical people Muggles.

Lightning-bolt shaped scar

WINGARDIUM LEVIOSA!

School tie in Gryffindor house colors

Wand made of holly wood

Harry at Hogwarts

When Harry turned eleven years old, he was invited to study at Hogwarts School of Witchcraft and Wizardry. It is a whole new world for Harry, filled with new friends, fascinating classes, and a whole castle full of magical wonders to explore!

Hogwarts castle

Hogwarts castle is located somewhere in Scotland, hidden away from Muggle eyes. British witches and wizards have been taught here for centuries. Students eat, sleep, and study within its ancient walls. Hogwarts is full of magic and mystery!

Harry's classmates

Harry soon makes friends at Hogwarts. His best friends are named Ron and Hermione. They are both in Gryffindor house, like Harry!

Ron Weasley comes from a large and friendly wizarding family. They all have bright red hair! Ron is good at wizard chess, but is afraid of spiders.

Hermione Granger's parents are both Muggles, but she knows a lot about magic and Hogwarts. She has learned it all from reading books!

Harry is not friends with Draco Malfoy. Draco is from a powerful wizarding family and thinks he is better than other students. He is in Slytherin house.

Hogwarts staff

Many clever witches and wizards teach classes at Hogwarts, led by Headmaster Albus Dumbledore.

WELCOME TO HOGWARTS!

Professor Dumbledore is very old but also very wise. He has watched over Harry since he was a baby. He knows Harry is a special young wizard.

Rubeus Hagrid looks after the Hogwarts grounds. He is kind and loyal, but can be clumsy. He is a half-giant, with a beard as big as his heart!

Professor Quirrell is Hogwarts' newest teacher. He teaches Defense Against the Dark Arts. He seems harmless but perhaps he has a dark side himself ...

Four houses

Every student in Hogwarts is sorted into a house. Brave Gryffindors are represented by lions, while wise Ravenclaw house has an eagle sign. Hardworking Hufflepuffs have a badger mascot. The snake symbol belongs to cunning Slytherin house.

BUILD YOUR OWN ADVENTURE

In the pages of this book, you will discover an exciting adventure and some clever ideas for LEGO® Harry Potter™ models. The models have been created by the LEGO Harry Potter design team at the LEGO Group headquarters in Billund, Denmark.

Use their models to inspire your own creations. If you don't have the perfect piece or your model doesn't look how you expected, try and find a creative solution. Chances are you can use your building skills to magically create something new. This is your adventure, so jump right in and start building!

ACCIO LEGO BRICKS!

BUILDER TALK

Did you know that LEGO® builders have their own language? You will find the terms below used a lot in this book. Here's what they mean:

MEASUREMENTS

LEGO pieces are described by the number of studs on them. If a brick has 2 studs across and 3 up, it's a 2x3 brick. If a piece is tall, it has a third number that is its height in standard bricks. Bricks are three times taller than LEGO plates.

3 plates = 1 brick

2x3 brick

1x1x5 brick

CLIP

Some pieces have clips on them. You can fit other elements into these clips. Pieces such as ladders fasten onto bars using built-in clips.

1x1 plate with clip

1x1 plate with clip

Ladder with two clips

BAR

Bars are useful for building long, thin features, but are also used with clips to create angles and moving parts. Bars are the perfect size to fit minifigure hands and some holes.

Bar

Staff

1x2 plate with bar

Bar with side studs

1x2 brick with bar

Stud with bar

TILE

When you want a smooth finish to your build, you need to use a tile. Printed tiles add extra detail to your models.

1x1 plate with shaft

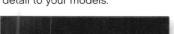

1x6 tile

2x2 tile

2x2 tile with pin

2x3 shield tile

SIDEWAYS BUILDING

Sometimes you need to build in two directions. That's when you need bricks or plates like these, with studs on more than one side.

1x4 brick with side studs

1x1 brick with two side studs

1x1 brick with one side stud

1x2/2x2 angle plate

1x8 plate with side rail

2x4 angled plate

PLATE

Like bricks, plates have studs on top and tubes on the bottom. However, plates are much thinner than bricks. Studs on jumper plates are placed slightly across to allow centered details.

1x2 jumper plate

2x4 plate

4x4 round plate

1x2 round plate with holes

4x4 curved plate

1x1 tooth plate

1x1 round plate

BRICK

Where would a builder be without the brick? It's the basis of most models and it comes in a huge variety of shapes and sizes.

1x2 textured brick

1x1 headlight brick

2x2 brick

2x2 domed brick

SLOPE

Slopes are bigger at the bottom than on top. Inverted slopes are the same, but upside down. They are smaller at the bottom and bigger on top.

1x2 slope

1x2 inverted slope

SPECIAL PIECES

Special pieces are used to create specific structures, or to link the build to a LEGO theme. Decorative pieces like these all work well in the LEGO Harry Potter world.

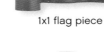

1x1 flag piece

1x2 printed letter tile

1x1 ice-cream piece

1x1 crystal piece

1x1 potion piece

Candle tube and flame

JOINT

If you want to make a roof that opens or give a creature a tail that moves, you need a moving part, such as a hinge or other joint.

2x2 brick with snap-joint connectors

Hinge plates

WHOO-WHOO!

Chapter 1
The Muggle world

Privet Drive

Harry Potter is just a baby when he is taken to live with his aunt and uncle. The great wizard Dumbledore has arranged for Harry to grow up with a family of Muggles (non-magical people) in an ordinary house. Even Harry won't know that he is a wizard.

WHAT AN ODD STREET!

Small radar dish

1x1 transparent yellow round brick

LEGO® connector is usually used to attach palm tree leaves

1x1 round brick

If you don't have a special lamp post piece for the base, you can use a pole on a jumper plate, or build a stack of 1x1 round bricks.

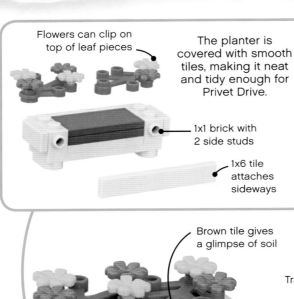

Flowers can clip on top of leaf pieces

The planter is covered with smooth tiles, making it neat and tidy enough for Privet Drive.

1x1 brick with 2 side studs

1x6 tile attaches sideways

Brown tile gives a glimpse of soil

Lamp post

Dumbledore doesn't want anyone to see him, so he turns out the street lights using magic. When he's completed his spell, you could swap out the yellow transparent brick for a clear one.

Top stud makes a good perch for an owl

Bulb lights up the street

Molded lamp post piece

LIGHTS OUT!

Transparent blue pieces make a gentle fountain

Slopes attach to a brick with side studs

Small base plate makes the tall model more stable

Front yard

Privet Drive residents are very house-proud and like their street to look neat and tidy. Add homely details like colorful flowers or a bird bath—strictly for non-magical creatures!

The Dursleys' house

Privet Drive is a very ordinary street in the town of Little Whinging. Harry's aunt and uncle don't like anything unusual. Their solid, sturdy house is built using nice, normal bricks, not with any magical funny business.

Chimney top is two double wall corner pieces

A 1x2 slope supports the chimney from below

Roof is edged with a 1x6 tile clipped sideways on angle plates

Hinged roof

The sloped roof attaches to the house with two hinges. 1x4 slope pieces on the side walls create a slanted support for the roof to sit on.

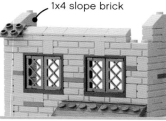

A hinge also creates a flat base for the chimney stack

Hinge piece sits at edge of wall

1x4 slope brick

Latticed window panes are popular in Little Whinging

Door lintel rests on hinges built into wall

Textured LEGO bricks are interspersed with colored plates to look like real stonework

MEOW!

A handful of green pieces make a small shrub

Lamp piece is clipped into the wall upside down

At the zoo

Harry grows up knowing nothing about the wizarding world, but that doesn't stop peculiar things happening when he's around. On a visit to the zoo, Harry discovers he can talk to snakes. He even sets one loose from its enclosure in the reptile house!

CAN ANYONE ELSE HEAR HISSING?

Burmese python, bred in captivity

1x3 slope brick raises the scene up so it's visible through the glass

REAR VIEW

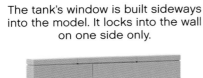

The tank's window is built sideways into the model. It locks into the wall on one side only.

Brick with side studs

1x4 tile does not attach to brown bricks

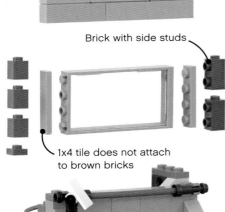

Window pane can pop out of the frame!

Plant piece with six stems

THAT ICCCE-CREAM LOOKSSS TASSSTY.

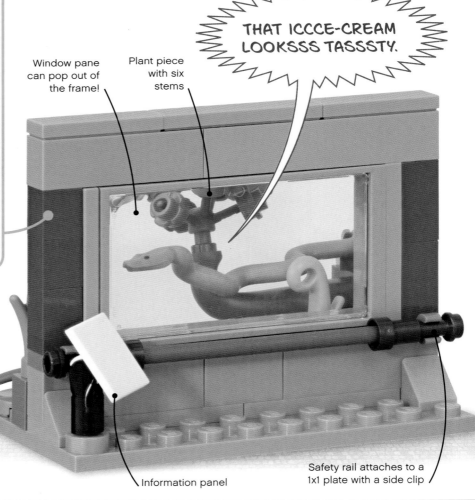

Snake house

Glass-fronted enclosures keep creatures and visitors safe, but only if the glass doesn't magically disappear! Create lush, natural habitats on one side of your model and add zoo details to the other.

Information panel

Safety rail attaches to a 1x1 plate with a side clip

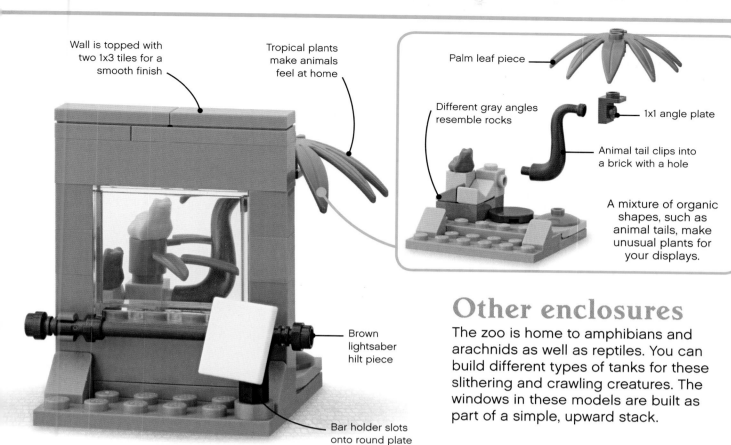

Wall is topped with two 1x3 tiles for a smooth finish

Tropical plants make animals feel at home

Palm leaf piece

Different gray angles resemble rocks

1x1 angle plate

Animal tail clips into a brick with a hole

A mixture of organic shapes, such as animal tails, make unusual plants for your displays.

Brown lightsaber hilt piece

Bar holder slots onto round plate with shaft

Other enclosures

The zoo is home to amphibians and arachnids as well as reptiles. You can build different types of tanks for these slithering and crawling creatures. The windows in these models are built as part of a simple, upward stack.

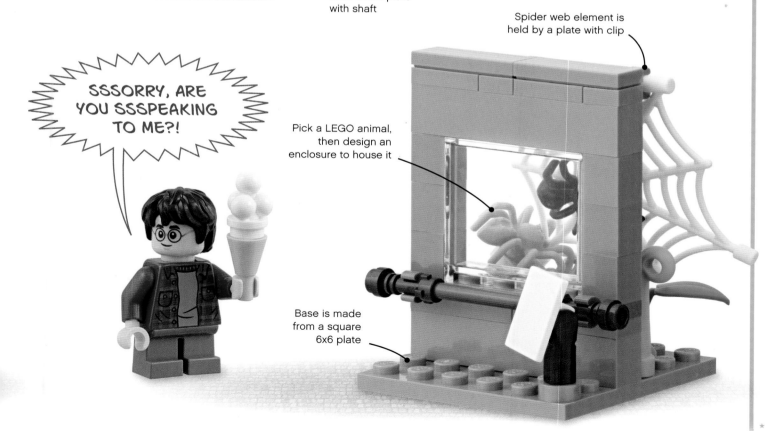

SSSORRY, ARE YOU SSSPEAKING TO ME?!

Spider web element is held by a plate with clip

Pick a LEGO animal, then design an enclosure to house it

Base is made from a square 6x6 plate

Harry's bedroom

At the Dursleys' house, Harry has to sleep in the cupboard under the stairs. This dark, cramped spot is the only space that his aunt and uncle will spare him. He makes the best of it with a simple bed and a reading light, but he doesn't have any toys to fill it with.

HOME SWEET HOME ...

A clip-and-bar connection creates an angled handrail

Spoon piece makes a bedside lamp

1x5x6 wall panel

1x1 gold stud for a door handle

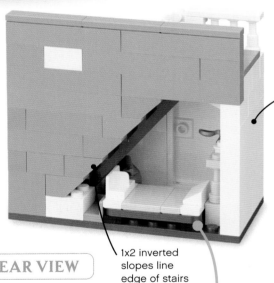

REAR VIEW

1x2 inverted slopes line edge of stairs

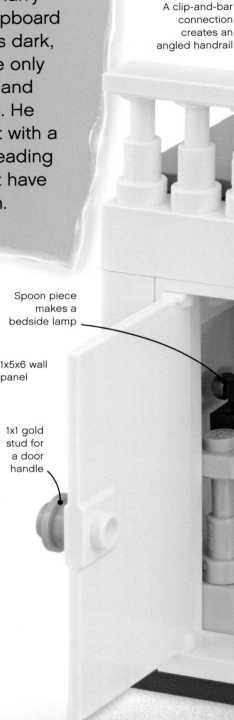

6x12 base plate

1x2 slope for pillow

1x3 jumper plate

LEGO® Technic 1x5 plate

1x5 plates are the perfect length for a short minifigure bed. A full-height minifigure would need a longer bed!

Tiles neaten up the top of the brick wall

Picture frame is attached to a brick with side studs

What will you build?
- Front door
- Dursleys' kitchen
- Hat stand

Cupboard under the stairs

This compact model is deliberately small on space! Leaving an open area in the back wall makes it easier to squeeze in a bed and shelves for Harry's few belongings. You could even add some spiders for company!

I WISH SOMEONE WOULD BUILD ME A REAL BEDROOM ...

Step-by-step

A pre-built stairway piece can be covered with colorful carpet. If you don't have this piece, you can easily construct your own stairs from 1x4 bricks and 2x4 plates.

1x4 edge plate

Stairway element

2x6 brick

Telescope pieces make elegant spindles

Plush wall-to-wall carpet covers the stairs

Mail delivery

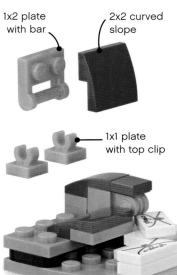

The mail doesn't usually come on Sundays, but letters addressed to Harry keep pouring into the Dursleys' house—even whizzing down the chimney! Despite there being so many letters, Harry hasn't been allowed to keep hold of one for long enough to actually read it.

I'VE GOT MAIL!

Fireplace

The key to this fireplace is a sliding mechanism that delivers a stream of letters through to the front of the model. The hole in the wall is framed by a carved surround.

Printed letter tiles can clip to studs or fly loose

Armchair

This comfy armchair is usually reserved just for Harry's uncle, but Harry uses it to try and reach the letters. Add to the scene by including a small reading lamp.

This luxurious armchair has no exposed studs, just curved slopes for plump, squashy cushions.

1x2 plate with bar

2x2 curved slope

1x1 plate with top clip

THESE CAN'T ALL BE BIRTHDAY CARDS!

Lampshade is a 2x2 round slope brick

LEGO pole piece

Lamp sits on a 1x1 plate with shaft

1x2 rounded plate

Brick with scroll supports armrest

Plain white 1x2 tiles also make good envelopes

Delivery chute

Bricks with grooves are used to control the flow of letters through the model. A box on the back of the wall has grooves that a tray can slot into. Pulling the tray out releases the letters stored on top.

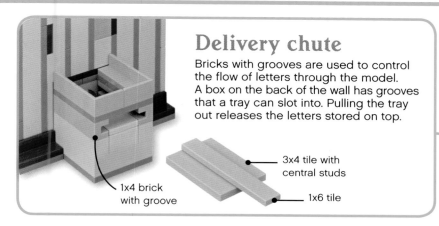

1x4 brick with groove

3x4 tile with central studs

1x6 tile

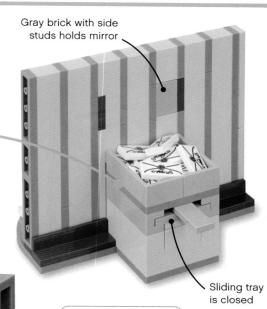

Gray brick with side studs holds mirror

REAR VIEW

Sliding tray is closed

Plates with side rails frame the mirror

Studs and stripes

Recreate the Dursleys' beige striped walls by building sideways in alternate layers of long bricks and plates. Plan ahead so the width of your wall matches the base plate.

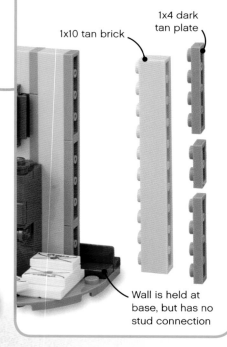

1x10 tan brick

1x4 dark tan plate

Wall is held at base, but has no stud connection

Letters fall through an open chute

Island hideout

YER A WIZARD, HARRY.

On the night before his eleventh birthday, Harry and his family are staying on a remote island because his uncle is trying to escape the magical stream of letters. Boom! Their tumbledown cottage shakes as a mysterious visitor arrives.

Birthday cake

Hagrid brings Harry a homemade birthday cake with bright pink icing. Cook up your own birthday build with any combination of tasty looking colors and shapes.

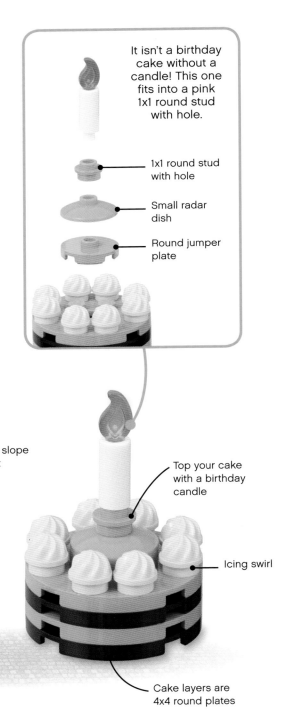

It isn't a birthday cake without a candle! This one fits into a pink 1x1 round stud with hole.

1x1 round stud with hole

Small radar dish

Round jumper plate

Top your cake with a birthday candle

Icing swirl

Cake layers are 4x4 round plates

Lumpy sofa

Harry isn't even allowed to sleep on the cottage's lumpy sofa. Luckily, a half-giant named Hagrid arrives with some exciting news: Harry is a wizard and has been invited to study at Hogwarts School of Witchcraft and Wizardry! Hagrid saves Harry from a night on the hard, dusty floor.

WHO ARE YOU??

1x2 curved half-arch brick

1x2 curved slope for armrest

2x8 plate makes an uncomfortable sleeping surface

Sofa foot is a 1x1 stud

Window is shut tight against the storm

Damp stonework

1x4 axle

Cuff

Small cog

Lever piece

Twisting the cog on the outside of the building moves the lever into the door. A narrow axle connects the two elements.

Smashing door

Hagrid sends the door of the island hideout flying, and you can, too. LEGO Technic pieces make a smashing mechanism that looks like real magic!

An upside-down lamp piece holds an open flame

1x2 brick with holes

SORRY ABOUT THAT!

Tile with two studs holds the door loosely, so it can be easily knocked out

1x2 slope

1x2 brick locks the fireplace into the wall

19

Chapter 2
The wizarding world

Diagon Alley

Pewter cauldrons, wands, and robes are not on most shopping lists, but they are vital school supplies for Harry. Luckily, Hagrid knows where to find them. Hidden from Muggle eyes, Diagon Alley is a busy shopping street, bustling with witches and wizards.

WE'RE IN THE MARKET FOR MAGIC!

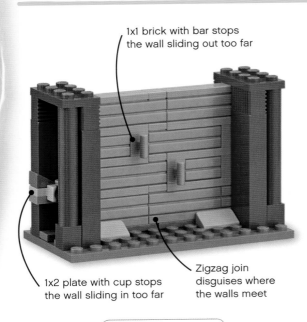

1x1 brick with bar stops the wall sliding out too far

1x2 plate with cup stops the wall sliding in too far

Zigzag join disguises where the walls meet

REAR VIEW

Secret entrance

This may look like a solid brick wall, but with the right magic, it melts away to reveal the way into Diagon Alley. Build a LEGO® wall with a sliding mechanism so minifigures can pass through.

I'M GLAD THAT WORKED.

Tiles on top of the wall help it glide under the top support

If you don't have pillar pieces, build supports from regular bricks

1x1 slope creates a handle

1x2 slope holds the wall in line

Walls run on smooth, narrow tiles

Ice cream parlor

Shops of all kinds line Diagon Alley, such as Florean Fortescue's Ice Cream Parlor. Attract shoppers to your own storefronts with dazzling window displays and giant signs.

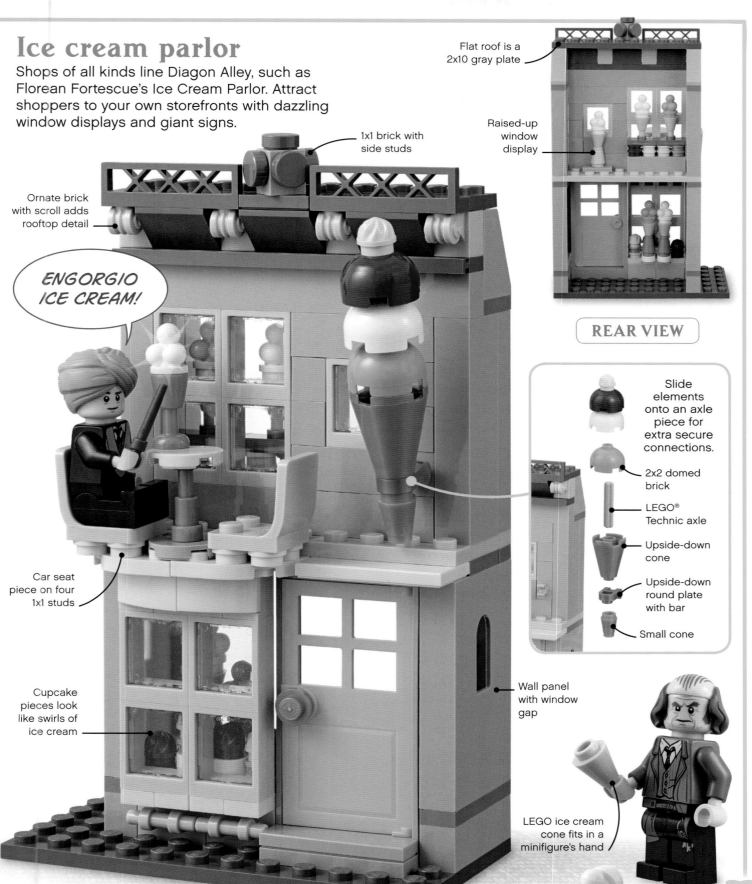

Flat roof is a 2x10 gray plate

Raised-up window display

1x1 brick with side studs

Ornate brick with scroll adds rooftop detail

ENGORGIO ICE CREAM!

REAR VIEW

Slide elements onto an axle piece for extra secure connections.

2x2 domed brick

LEGO® Technic axle

Upside-down cone

Upside-down round plate with bar

Small cone

Car seat piece on four 1x1 studs

Wall panel with window gap

Cupcake pieces look like swirls of ice cream

LEGO ice cream cone fits in a minifigure's hand

Gringotts bank

The stores in Diagon Alley don't take regular Muggle money. Fortunately for Harry, there is a huge fortune waiting for him in Gringotts, the wizard bank. However, Hagrid and Harry must face a wild and winding path before they strike wizarding gold!

THIS IS THE BEST DAY EVER!

Small details transform this roller coaster car into a robust mining cart. Remember, a Gringotts cart doesn't need a working steering wheel—it is controlled by magic!

Steering wheel

Wrench piece

1x2 plate with bar

Headlight brick

Bumper is a 1x4 double curved slope

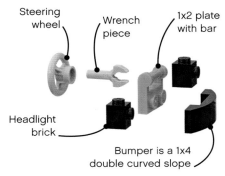

Bank cart

Gringotts stretches deep underground. The best way to get around the vaults is by rail. These molded roller coaster rails and car pieces send Harry speeding on his way!

THE CART DRIVES ITSELF, HARRY!

SLOW DOWN, HAGRID!

Gold 1x4 fence piece

Each molded car has a bar at the front and a clip at the back

These decorative wheels don't spin; the cart's functioning wheels run inside the rails

Bank tunnel

Gringotts' tunnels are carved through underground rocks and caves. Building a flat wall with a round hole gives the impression of a tunnel, without having to build the whole thing!

Slopes and inverted slopes in a variety of sizes and angles make craggy rocks

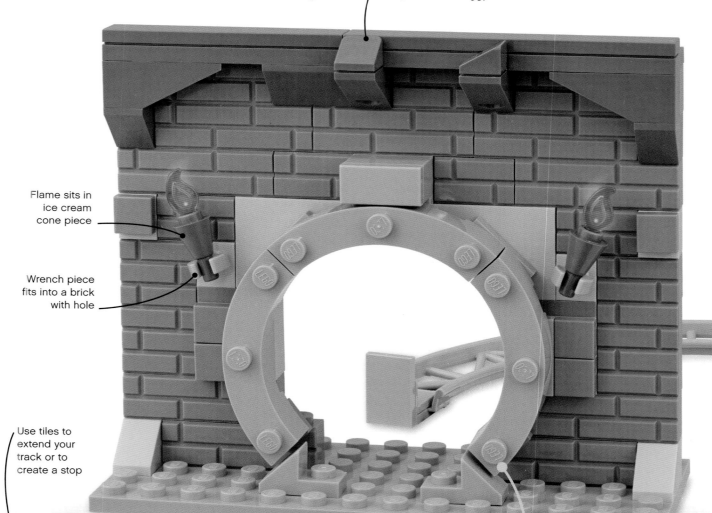

Flame sits in ice cream cone piece

Wrench piece fits into a brick with hole

Use tiles to extend your track or to create a stop

Hundreds of miles of track line Gringotts tunnels

Trick of the eye

It is surprisingly simple to turn a square hole into a round one. Include bricks with sides studs at the edges of your wall, then overlay with curved bricks for a round tunnel shape.

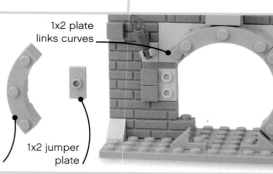

1x2 plate links curves

4x4 quarter ring

1x2 jumper plate

In the vaults

Witches and wizards store their valuables in Gringotts bank for good reason. Its high-security vaults are protected with the usual locks and bolts, but also enchantments, curses, and (rumor has it) a dragon. Who knows what treasures lurk inside these walls?

YER RICH, HARRY!

Intricate detailing makes these doors look tough to crack, but each one swings open on a simple bar-and-clip connection.

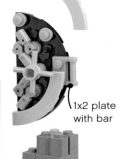

Brick with clip

1x2 plate with bar

Bar holder clips to 1x1 plate with shaft

Harry's vault

Each customer has their own vault with a magical goblin-made lock. Build one with round, hinged doors large enough for even Hagrid to walk through.

Hub piece with four bars makes a locking wheel

WHERE DID I PUT MY KEYS?

Half arches and inverted half arches create a circular hole

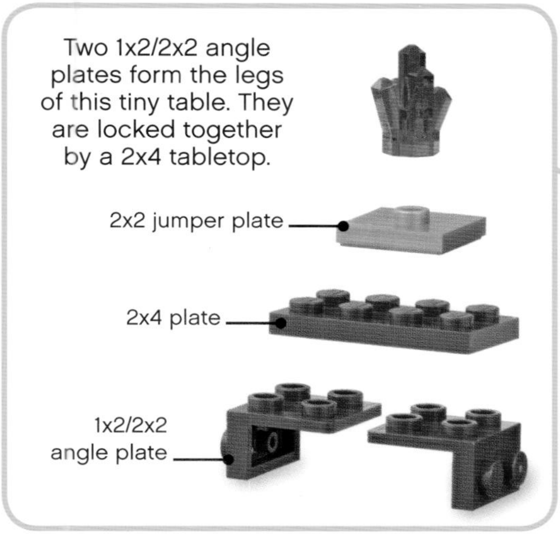
Two 1x2/2x2 angle plates form the legs of this tiny table. They are locked together by a 2x4 tabletop.
2x2 jumper plate
2x4 plate
1x2/2x2 angle plate

Sorcerer's Stone

Hagrid collects an item for Professor Dumbledore. The top-secret Sorcerer's Stone is a magical object that can bestow eternal life. Dumbledore wants to keep it safe at Hogwarts.

What will you build?

- Treasure chests
- Booby traps
- Dragon's nest

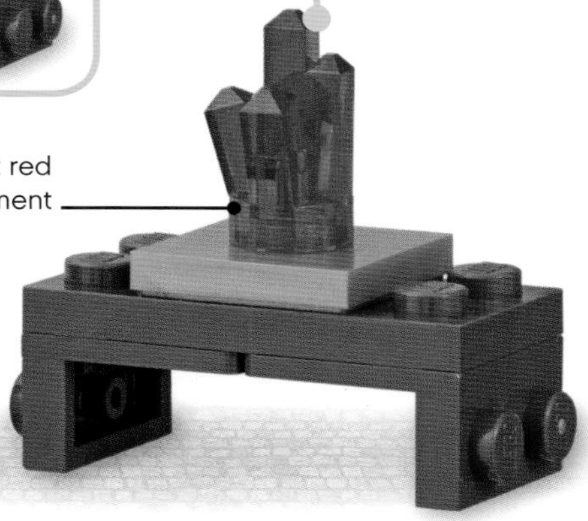
Transparent red crystal element

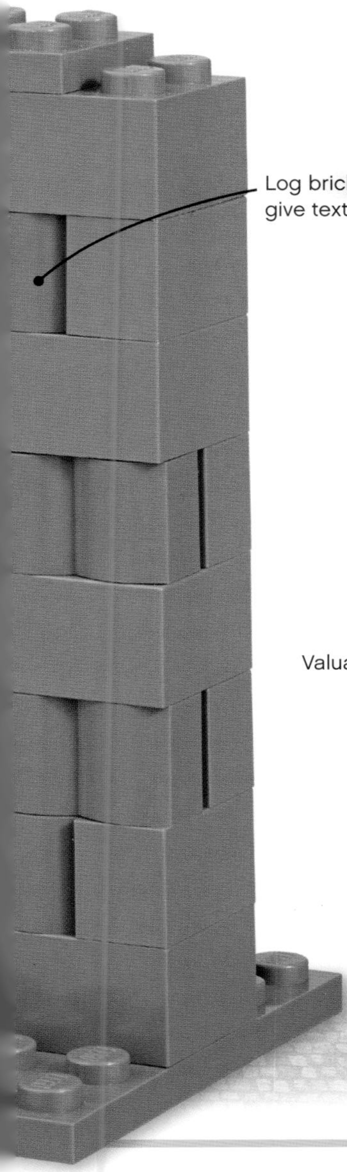
Log bricks give texture

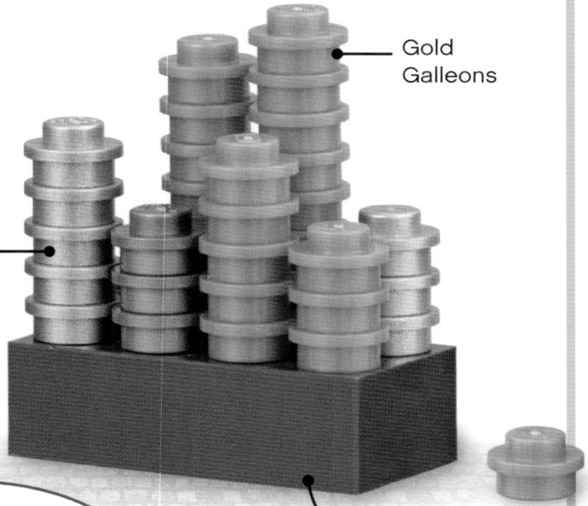
Gold Galleons
Silver Sickles
Solid 2x4 brick makes a simple table

Harry's treasure

In vault 687, Harry discovers more money than he has ever seen in his life. Use metallic LEGO pieces to create all sorts of treasures for him.

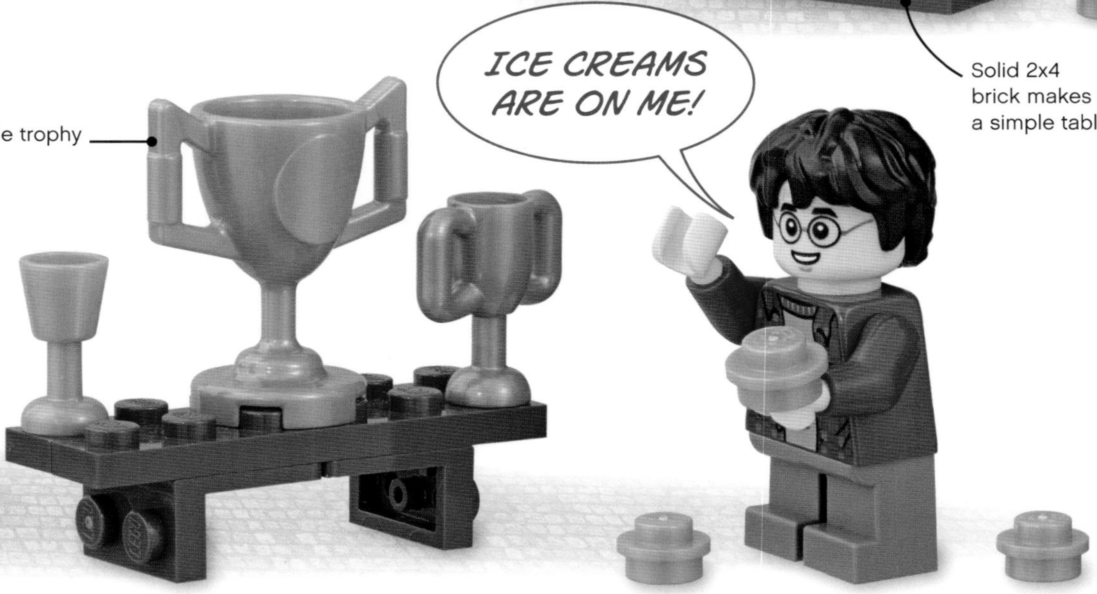
Valuable trophy
ICE CREAMS ARE ON ME!

Ollivander's shop

A wizard doesn't choose their wand—the wand chooses the wizard. This shop might look old-fashioned, but Ollivander's: Makers of Fine Wands Since 382 BC is world famous. Harry is certainly in the right place to try his first ever wand!

AH! PLEASE DO COME IN, MR. POTTER!

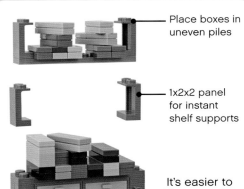

Place boxes in uneven piles

1x2x2 panel for instant shelf supports

It's easier to fill your LEGO shelves before you stack them.

Wand shelves

Ollivander's has more stock than you could wave a wand at. Narrow boxes line shelves all the way up to the ceiling. Build a ladder so Mr. Ollivander can reach them all.

Ladder piece with two clips

Wand boxes are built with plates and tiles

IS IT SUPPOSED TO DO THAT?

1x4 bar stabilizes the ladder

Drawers for even more wands

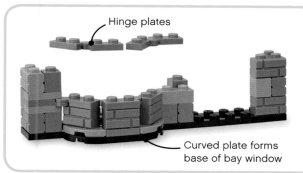

Hinge plates

Curved plate forms base of bay window

Angled window

The three-sided bay window is created with pairs of overlapping hinge plates. Once you have the right shape, just start stacking windows on top!

What will you build?

- The Leaky Cauldron pub
- Owl emporium
- Magical book store

Rotate some textured bricks so the effect continues on the sides of your model

Hinge plates secure the top of the bay window

Wand held in a 1x1 tile with top clip

1x2 plate with bar supports the sign

Storefront

Ollivander's has stood on Diagon Alley for hundreds of years. The yellowing windows look like they aren't cleaned very often, but a simple standing sign makes it clear what is sold inside.

Chapter 3
Welcome to Hogwarts

Hogwarts castle

Welcome to Hogwarts School of Witchcraft and Wizardry! Hogwarts students are taught magical subjects like Potions, Herbology, and Charms by wise teachers. Hogwarts is a jumble of towers, turrets, and secret passages, all held together by magic.

HAVE YOU READ HOGWARTS: A HISTORY?

A 1x4 plate locks two half-arch pieces together. Build arch sides symmetrically so they meet neatly at the top.

2x2/1x2 angle plate

1x4 plate

1x4 slope

Half arch

If you don't have large door pieces, you can build them out of plates

Doorway

Hogwarts is an ancient castle, full of stone arches, high ceilings, and ornate carvings. Build some grand wooden doors three times the height of a minifigure.

Round transparent orange plates add bulk to the flaming torches

2x2 inverted slope brick

VERY NICE TO MEET YOU BOTH.

1x1x6 round column piece gives the stone wall texture

4x4 round brick

Stairway element

4x4 turntable element

Spinning stairs

Each flight of stairs in this model spins on a large turntable piece. It means two flights can turn in different directions at the same time.

WHICH WAY IS IT TO DINNER NOW?

Molded staircase piece gives model extra stability

Staircase

Hogwarts' staircases can move by themselves, so students need to keep their wits about them when traveling around the castle. Start building this model and who knows where you'll end up!

What will you build?
- Hogwarts corridors
- The Owlery
- Hagrid's hut

Overlapping 1x2 curved half arches

Small slopes for bust's shoulders

All-gray minifigure looks like a suit of armor

The crossed base keeps the model balanced, whichever way the stairs swivel

Sorting Ceremony

There are four Hogwarts houses: Gryffindor, Ravenclaw, Hufflepuff, and Slytherin. The first thing new students experience is the Sorting Ceremony. Each student wears the Sorting Hat on their head and waits for it to declare which house they will join.

NOT SLYTHERIN, EH?

House points

Pupils earn points for their houses with their triumphs, but rule-breaking loses points. A running total is kept, and at the end of the year, whichever house has the most points wins the House Cup.

Build a house-point counter to keep track of each house's points. Change the colors of bricks in the columns below when the scores change.

2x2 round inverted tile

Upside-down 2x2 round plate

Upside-down hollow dome piece

GRYFFINDOR!

Harry takes his turn under the Sorting Hat

House-point counters yet to be earned

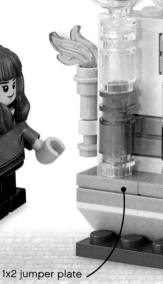

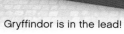

The spinner has stopped on Gryffindor!

1x2 jumper plate

Gryffindor is in the lead!

House colors

Students show their house pride in many different ways. The castle is decorated with brightly colored banners and flags. Here are some different techniques for constructing decorations, but you could come up with many more.

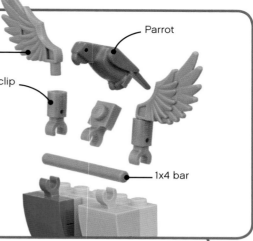

Feathered wing element

Parrot

Bar holder with clip

1x4 bar

Transfiguration

Transform a parrot piece into Ravenclaw's majestic eagle mascot. The bird's body is not attached to its wings, but sits very close to them. Hold it all tight in place with clips.

Layers of tiles and plates create a checkerboard design

HUFFLEPUFF

GRYFFINDOR

Waving flag element is used sideways

2x3 curved plate with hole

Mixture of bars, clips, and tall bricks makes a frame for a tapestry

Plates are linked by a red 2x6 plate at the back

Transparent pole holds up "floating" banner

2x2 curved slope

MY FATHER SAYS SLYTHERIN IS BEST.

Two angled plates look like a forked snake's tongue

Pointed shield tile

SLYTHERIN

RAVENCLAW

Teachers' table

Hogwarts students eat together in the magnificent Great Hall. Huge platters of delicious food are prepared in the kitchens, then magically appear on the long wooden dining tables. The teachers sit at a large table at the top of the dining hall.

DINNER IS SERVED!

Dumbledore's chair

As headmaster, Dumbledore gets the grandest chair. It has gold details, a green trim, and stately arms.

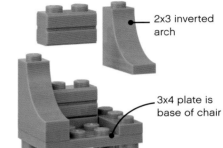

Gold 1x1 cone

2x3 inverted arch

3x4 plate is base of chair

Gold 1x1 round brick

Top table

This table shows two techniques for building table legs. As well as raising the tabletop, the central legs link two LEGO® plates together to make a long surface.

WHO HAS STOLEN MY PIZZA?

Lay the table with LEGO food elements or use round tiles as empty plates

1x2 brick connects the plates above

NEARLY HEADLESS NICK, AT YOUR SERVICE.

What will you build?

- Food platters
- Stone carvings
- Stained glass windows

Gold lectern

Dumbledore addresses the school from his gleaming lectern. Remember: the third-floor corridor on the right-hand side is out of bounds to everyone!

Candle tube

Upside-down round 1x1 plate

Upside-down 1x1 plate with top clip

1x4 bar

Standing tall

The intricate lectern is built around a 1x1 brick with side studs. A bar is attached to the back of the brick, with candles added using upside-down connections.

ERRM ... NOT ME?

Ice cream element in a goblet

Gold flame element

Roller-skate piece

Stand is a goblet piece

1x4 arch

Log bricks form chair legs

Dumbledore stands on a podium to speak

Common room

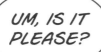

The Gryffindor common room is a cozy place to kick back and relax. Students spend lots of their free time here, catching up on homework, chatting, and playing games like wizard chess. Only Gryffindors are allowed inside, though. No password means no entry!

WHAT'S THE PASSWORD?

Layers of art

The portrait is built in three layers. The backdrop is a wall with a colored scene. Next, a one-brick-wide stone surround gives depth. The front layer features a hole and picture frame for the Fat Lady to sit in.

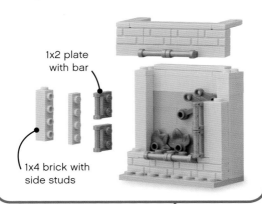

1x2 plate with bar

1x4 brick with side studs

Fat Lady portrait

The Fat Lady is a moving, speaking oil painting who guards the door to the Gryffindor common room. The easiest way to make a minifigure picture is simply to use a minifigure!

UM, IS IT PLEASE?

Center of the wall is hollow

Plates with bars form a golden picture frame

Leafy background detail

WRONG AGAIN!

Godric Gryffindor

Harry's house is named after Godric Gryffindor. He was a great wizard and one of the four founders of Hogwarts. Why not build a white marble bust in his honor?

Plates make a great flat base for a sofa, but the studs don't look very comfy. Red tiles clip onto the seat and along the backrest, for a less bumpy seat.

1x4 brick with side studs

2x2 red tile

Round plates for decoration

White minifigure hair piece

I'VE READ ABOUT YOU.

1x2 half arch rounds off the backrest

Round grooved brick makes a sturdy plinth

Cushions sit loose on sofa

Cozy sofa

After a long day of studying, there's nothing better than snuggling up on one of the common room's comfy sofas. This one uses Gryffindor house colors, but you could build one for any house.

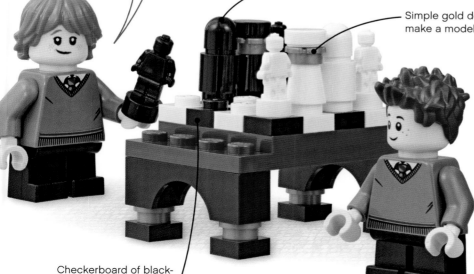

THAT'S WIZARD CHESS!

Light bulb element

Simple gold details can make a model look grand

Wizard chess

Use a variety of small elements to create your own chess pieces. They can then be broken apart when they are captured—just like in real wizard chess!

Checkerboard of black-and-white 1x1 plates

Dormitory

Harry has a lot to learn about being a wizard, so life at Hogwarts is very busy. He is exhausted at the end of each day. He and Ron sleep in a dormitory in Gryffindor Tower. There are no teachers, no pesky ghosts, and, best of all, no Slytherins!

THIS ROOM IS A DREAM COME TRUE!

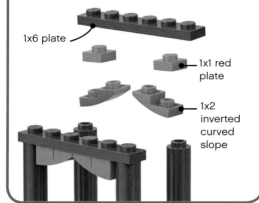

Attach a canopy to the bottom of the bed railings. Inverted curved slopes create the draped shape of the curtains. Leave a space at each end to connect the bedposts.

1x6 plate

1x1 red plate

1x2 inverted curved slope

Four-poster bed

Harry's impressive four-poster bed is a huge upgrade from his bed under the stairs at Privet Drive. It isn't complicated to build though, just add a tall frame around a simple bed build.

WHY ARE YOU STANDING ON THE BED?

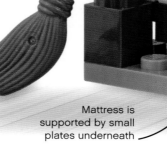

Decorative plates sit in each corner

If you don't have any column pieces, you can stack small bricks

Nimbus 2000 broomstick was a gift

Mattress is supported by small plates underneath

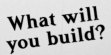

What will you build?

- Storage trunks
- Bedside table
- Window seat

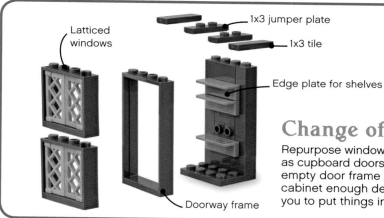

Latticed windows

1x3 jumper plate

1x3 tile

Edge plate for shelves

Doorway frame

Change of use

Repurpose window pieces as cupboard doors. An empty door frame gives the cabinet enough depth for you to put things inside.

Storage cupboard

Harry has never owned this much stuff! Build him a cupboard to keep his books, clothes, wand, and other wizarding items tidy.

Harry's owl, Hedwig

MOUSE! ... OH, IT'S JUST SCABBERS.

Window elements open like cupboard doors

Golden snitch element

Ron's rat, Scabbers

Patchwork quilt

Chapter 4
Life at Hogwarts

Potions class

Harry and Hermione are in the Potions classroom brewing magical mixtures that can cure boils, make people forgetful, or even counter dangerous poisons. Harry doesn't enjoy the class, though. It is taught by grumpy Professor Snape, head of Slytherin house.

I CAN BOTTLE FAME AND BREW GLORY.

Burning build

Potions are simmered over burners like those used in laboratories. Only one leg of the model connects to the table.

LEGO® Technic half pin

Upside-down plate with four bars

Upside-down 2x2 round tile

Work benches

Students work at benches of all shapes and sizes. Just make sure you have a flat, stable surface before you add your concoctions!

WHAT DO I DO NOW, HERMIONE?

Spilled potion bottle is held by plate with top clip

1x1 plate with hole holds burner in place

Saucepan element

Ice cream element looks like a bubbling potion

Quill for taking notes

Black inkwell is a 1x1 plate with shaft

Window frames make stable legs

44

Supply shelves

Potion-making requires many curious ingredients, including dragon's blood, puffapods, and wolfsbane. Combine shapes and colors for a variety of intriguing-looking containers and lids.

Jewel-piece stopper

Colored conical flask

Use ordinary bricks to separate the shelves if you don't have window panes

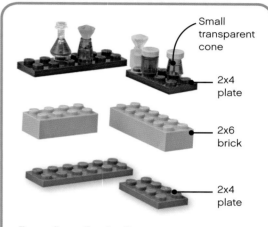

Small transparent cone

2x4 plate

2x6 brick

2x4 plate

Locked tight

This corner unit is firmly locked together by overlapping plates and bricks at its base. Alternate different length pieces so the joins are held tightly by pieces above and below.

Candle stands in a flower piece with a hole

2x3 slope brick

Use telescope pieces for legs

THAT'S MINUS TEN HOUSE POINTS, MR. POTTER.

What will you build?

- Astronomy tower
- Charms classroom
- Herbology greenhouse

Snape's desk

Professor Snape has an old-fashioned desk, with an angled writing surface. He can stand behind it to teach, grade homework, or quiz his students with difficult questions.

Flying lessons

Harry's favorite activity at Hogwarts is flying broomsticks! First-years are taught to fly by Madam Hooch. Harry is a naturally excellent flyer, which annoys another student, Draco Malfoy. Harry is soon racing Draco around the Hogwarts grounds!

CATCH ME IF YOU CAN, POTTER!

Stone bridge

Madam Hooch watches her flying students from a high point in the grounds—a stone bridge. Minifigures on broomsticks can fly over, under, or around the bridge!

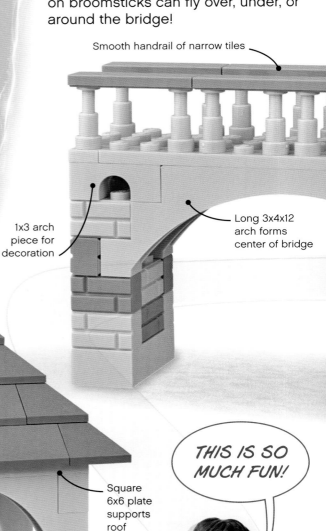

Smooth handrail of narrow tiles

1x3 arch piece for decoration

Long 3x4x12 arch forms center of bridge

Courtyard

Flying lessons take place in a grassy courtyard with plenty of room to practice maneuvering. Build different features of the castle grounds and create an obstacle course for Harry and his friends to explore.

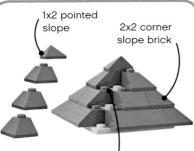

1x2 pointed slope

2x2 corner slope brick

Hidden bricks can be any color

Pointed top

This steeply angled roof is built up layer by layer. At each stage, a square of yellow bricks is surrounded by gray slopes. The levels get smaller as they go up, finally ending with two pointed slopes.

Square 6x6 plate supports roof

THIS IS SO MUCH FUN!

Round brick makes pillars look carved

Two-tone stone statue

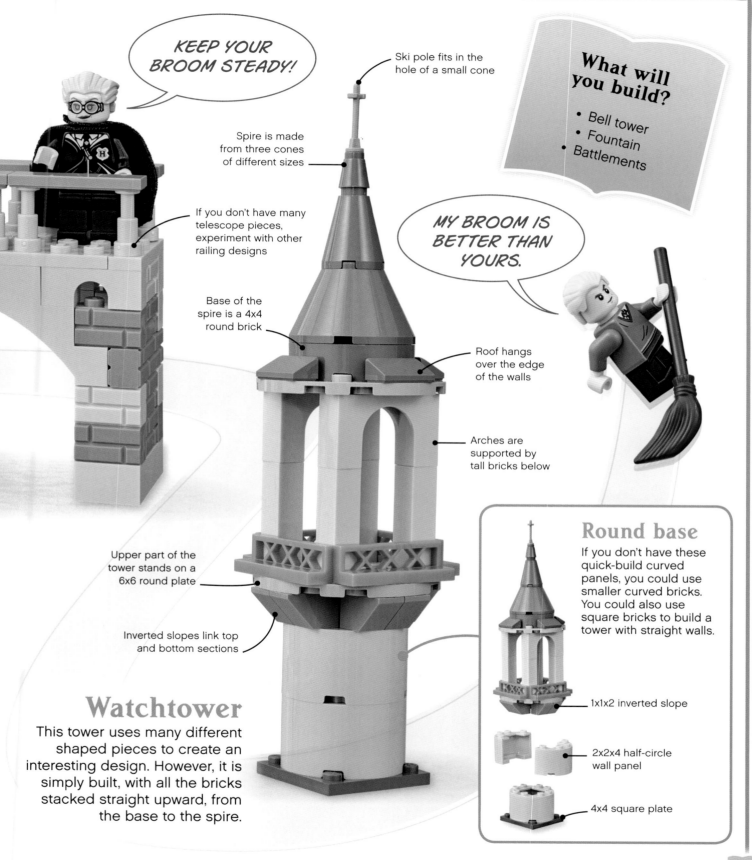

KEEP YOUR BROOM STEADY!

Ski pole fits in the hole of a small cone

What will you build?

- Bell tower
- Fountain
- Battlements

Spire is made from three cones of different sizes

If you don't have many telescope pieces, experiment with other railing designs

MY BROOM IS BETTER THAN YOURS.

Base of the spire is a 4x4 round brick

Roof hangs over the edge of the walls

Arches are supported by tall bricks below

Upper part of the tower stands on a 6x6 round plate

Inverted slopes link top and bottom sections

Round base

If you don't have these quick-build curved panels, you could use smaller curved bricks. You could also use square bricks to build a tower with straight walls.

1x1x2 inverted slope

2x2x4 half-circle wall panel

4x4 square plate

Watchtower

This tower uses many different shaped pieces to create an interesting design. However, it is simply built, with all the bricks stacked straight upward, from the base to the spire.

Library visit

Students are expected to stay in their dormitories after dark. Filch, the caretaker, keeps watch for anyone who is out of bed. Harry hides under an Invisibility Cloak while he explores the restricted section of the library. But he isn't the only person sneaking around ...

I KNOW YOU'RE THERE!

Delicate detail

Only the two vine pieces attach to the arch. Everything else sits on top of the fence. A bar with side studs allows detail to go out to the side, as well as up.

Flower with hole

Bar with side studs

1x2 jumper plate

THERE'S A STUDENT OUT OF BED, MRS. NORRIS ...

MEOW!

Window frame

Hogwarts window panes have grand designs between pieces of glass. This one looks complicated, but it is surprisingly simple to assemble.

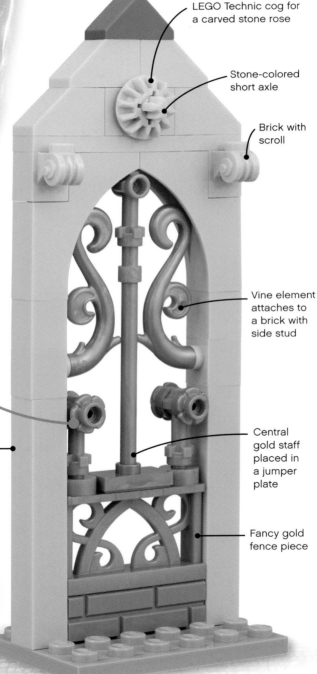

LEGO Technic cog for a carved stone rose

Stone-colored short axle

Brick with scroll

Vine element attaches to a brick with side stud

Central gold staff placed in a jumper plate

Fancy gold fence piece

1x1x5 tall brick

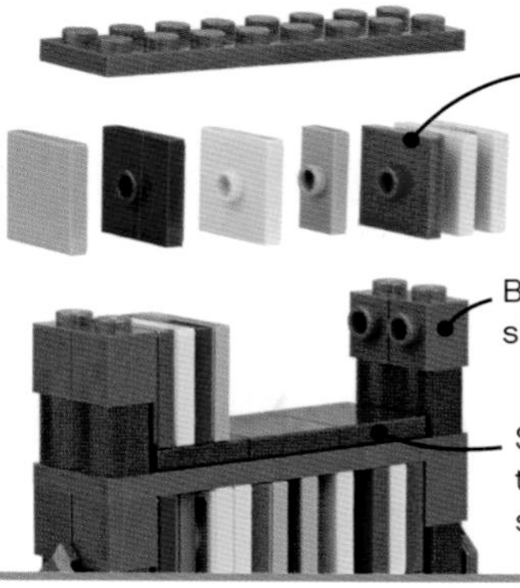

Robot arm holds book

Row of handled bars

2x2 jumper plate

Side stack

This row of books stands so straight because all the books connect to each other. Join a group of sideways plates together, then clip them as a block to the sides of the bookcase.

Brick with side studs

Smooth tiles line shelf

Reading lamp

Hinged brick

Edge plate holds book in place

Bookshelves

Hogwarts has a huge collection of wizarding books. Ancient, leather-bound texts fill the wooden shelves. Dangerous books of Dark magic are kept out of reach of students and locked up with chains.

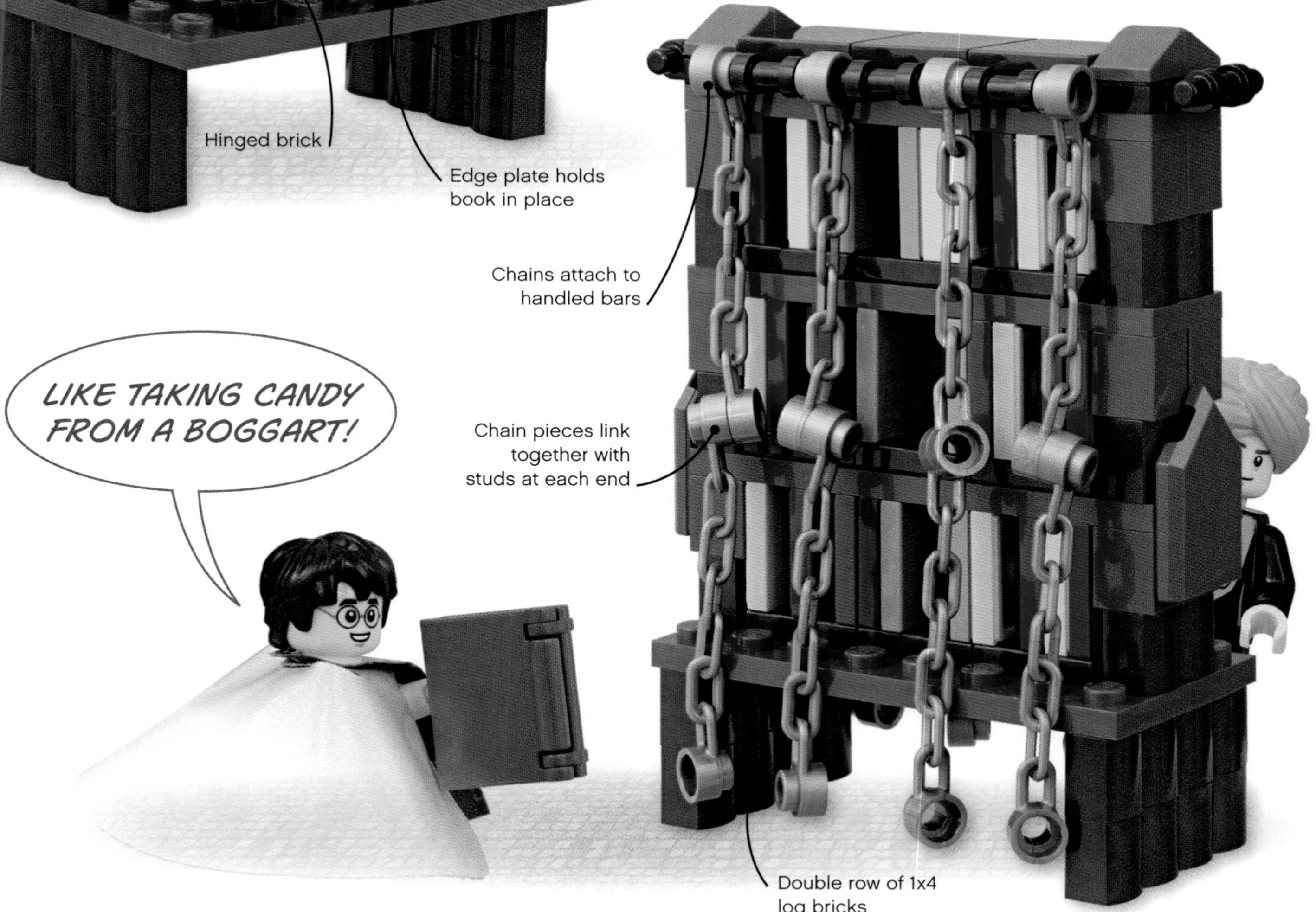

Chains attach to handled bars

Chain pieces link together with studs at each end

LIKE TAKING CANDY FROM A BOGGART!

Double row of 1x4 log bricks

Halloween feast

Happy Halloween! October 31 is a special day at Hogwarts. The Great Hall is decorated with magical floating pumpkins. Students, teachers, and ghosts share in the excitement as the school gathers for an elaborate Halloween feast!

DO I NEED A COSTUME?

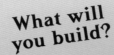

What will you build?

- Decorations
- Skeletons
- Creepy carriage

WHAT A DAY TO BE ALIVE!

Fireplace is decorated for Halloween

Feasting table

There is always plenty of food at Hogwarts, but on feast days the tables are even more full than usual. Fill your Halloween scene with delicious sweet treats, but watch out for tricks!

Pumpkin pie

Cauldron-style serving dish filled with food

Pie stand is a round jumper plate

Pupils sit on long benches to eat

Floating pumpkins

The ceiling in the Great Hall is normally bewitched to resemble the sky outside. However, at Halloween it's filled with carved pumpkins, enchanted to float above the diners' heads.

Alternating sized slope pieces leaves gaps for transparent supports

Half-arch piece juts out into the room

The pole clips into the hole in a 1x1 brick with side stud

Floating pumpkin clips to a clear pole with plate

Wall-mounted fire is called a brazier

The brazier's octagonal base clips onto the wall sideways, but the vertical elements make it look like it is hanging.

Skeleton leg piece

Octagonal ring element

1x2 plate with side clip

Lattice windows are traditional castle features

MY TALKING PUMPKIN CHARM WENT WRONG ...

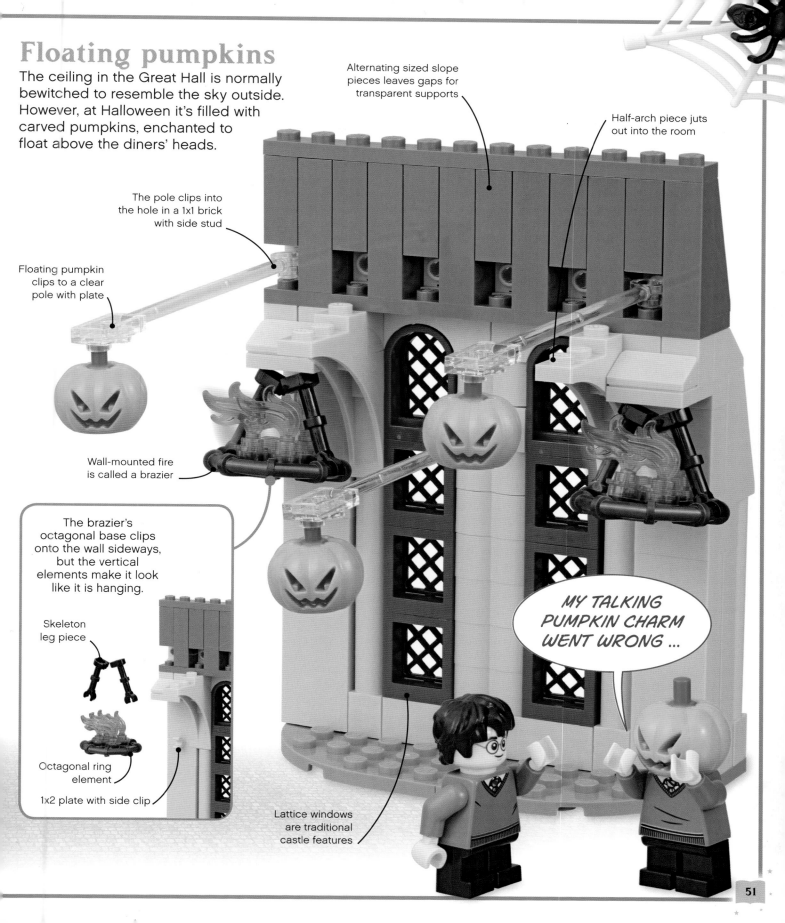

Chapter 5
Magical adventures

Forbidden Forest

Within Hogwarts' grounds is a dark, eerie forest—home to many mysterious and dangerous creatures. It's normally out of bounds to students. When they get detention, Harry and Draco are sent to help Hagrid, the gamekeeper, patrol the forest.

WHO KNOWS WHAT LURKS IN THERE ...

What will you build?

- Log cabin
- Fallen tree trunk
- Unicorn

THERE'S NOTHING SCARIER IN HERE THAN A MALFOY.

WAIT UNTIL MY FATHER HEARS ABOUT THIS ...

Winding path

Alternate plates with different types of curved edges to make a twisting path. Small green pieces link the brown plates and look like mossy growth on the forest floor.

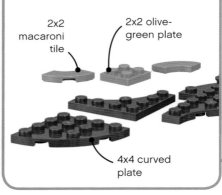

2x2 macaroni tile

2x2 olive-green plate

4x4 curved plate

Forest path

Harry and Draco have to carefully find their way along a winding path. Build a few small sections and arrange them to give the impression of a much longer path.

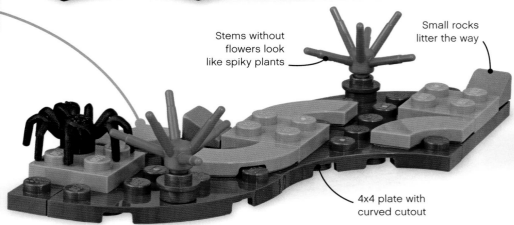

Stems without flowers look like spiky plants

Small rocks litter the way

4x4 plate with curved cutout

Gnarled trees

The forest is full of trees growing in twisted shapes as they search for light in the gloom. These spindly trees are built in sideways layers. Try building them flat, then standing them upright.

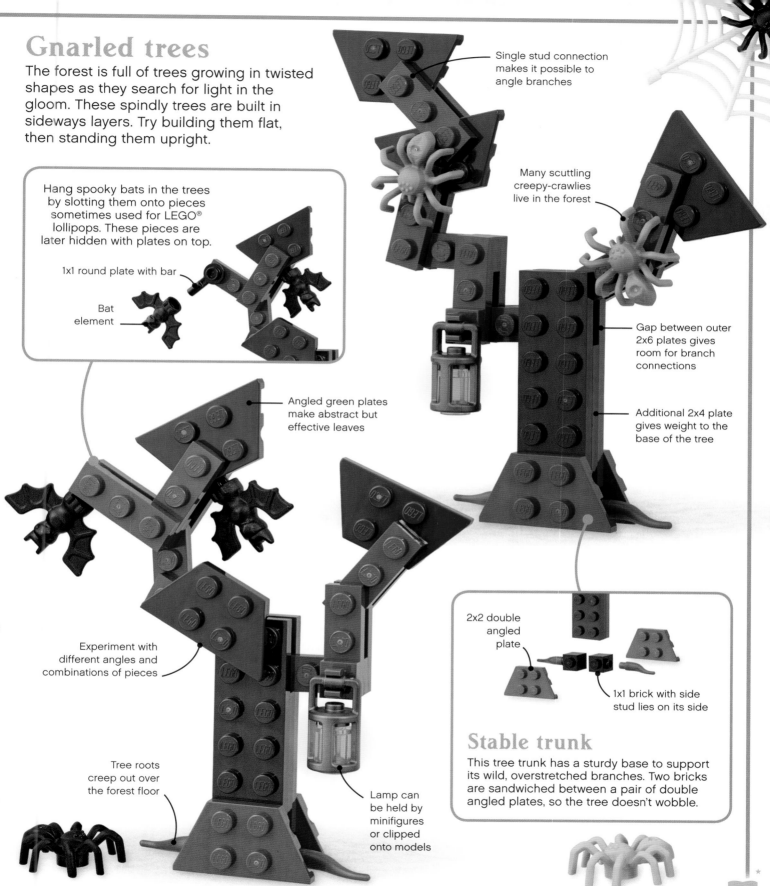

Single stud connection makes it possible to angle branches

Many scuttling creepy-crawlies live in the forest

Gap between outer 2x6 plates gives room for branch connections

Additional 2x4 plate gives weight to the base of the tree

Hang spooky bats in the trees by slotting them onto pieces sometimes used for LEGO® lollipops. These pieces are later hidden with plates on top.

1x1 round plate with bar

Bat element

Angled green plates make abstract but effective leaves

Experiment with different angles and combinations of pieces

Tree roots creep out over the forest floor

Lamp can be held by minifigures or clipped onto models

2x2 double angled plate

1x1 brick with side stud lies on its side

Stable trunk

This tree trunk has a sturdy base to support its wild, overstretched branches. Two bricks are sandwiched between a pair of double angled plates, so the tree doesn't wobble.

Troll attack

TROLL! Troll in the dungeon! While the school is enjoying a feast, someone lets a fierce, dim-witted troll into Hogwarts. The huge troll staggers his way from the dungeons up to the girls' bathroom. Can Ron, Harry, and Hermione use their magic to defeat it?

WHAT'S THAT NOISE?

Bathroom sink

Hogwarts plumbing is functional, but not very fancy. This large white sink is built into the wall, so remember to include white bricks for it as you construct the gray tiled wall.

Mirror is attached to a brick with side studs

1x2 white slopes are built into wall

Exposed water pipes are upturned tap elements

Toilet stall

Hermione discovers that a toilet stall is not a good hiding place—the troll can easily smash through its thin walls and door. This stall has an old-fashioned toilet with an overhead cistern.

Upside-down 1x1 round plate

The seat and pipe hover over the toilet bowl without touching it. The black pieces are held in place by a clip in the wall, while the white section attaches to the floor.

Upside-down antenna piece

Life buoy element with stud

Inverted dome piece

1x2 jumper plate

Raised water tank is built around a brick with side studs

Stall door swings on clip-and-bar hinges

WINGARDIUM LEVIOSA!

Walls are raised on stacked 1x1 plates

Flying piece
of toilet stall

Troll

Trolls are vicious creatures
with huge strength but
tiny brains. Experiment
with different ways to
build one. Don't forget a
lumpy body; bulging belly;
and thick, muscular limbs.

1x2 curved slope
with a point

The troll's blocky
head sits on a
jumper plate so
it can turn all the
way around.
Watch out, Harry!

1x2 jumper plate

Mouth is two 1x2
plates with side rails

Shoulder is a
tooth on a plate

What will
you build?

- Dungeons
- Broken pipes
- Troll trap

ARGH!

Limbs are
covered with 1x2
curved slopes

Loincloth is a 2x2
angled plate

Hip has a
cup-and-
ball joint

Small round tiles
make knobbly knees

Ball joint
at end
of leg

1x2 plate
with cup

1x1 semi-
circle tile

Stinky feet

The troll stomps on two large
feet. Layer up plates sideways
to make a flat foot with toenails.
Include half of a ball-and-cup
socket joint in each foot so you
can attach it to the leg.

Big toe has an extra
plate behind it

Facing Fluffy

Harry, Ron, and Hermione suspect someone is trying to steal the Sorcerer's Stone. They try to follow the thief, but are blocked by a vicious three-headed guard dog! The creature, named Fluffy, has just been woken up from a nap—and he isn't happy!

WE MUST PROTECT THE STONE!

WOOF!

Swiveling head

Fluffy's heads can turn to follow the gang no matter which way they flee. Each head is connected using a ball-and-cup joint and has a simple chain collar.

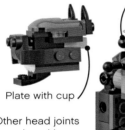

2x2 plate with ball

Plate with cup

Other head joints are placed lower

ARF!

Lower jaw is an inverted curved slope

I'M MORE OF A CAT PERSON!

RUFF!

Each claw is a horn piece in a round stud with hole

Each of Fluffy's heads is identical. They are all structured around a block of three bricks with side studs. Build them up with bricks in all directions.

Transparent green eyes

Curved slope brick looks like nostrils

1x2 plate with teeth

Bricks sit on 2x3 plate

Pointy ear is a tooth plate

Tail piece clips into a brick with hole

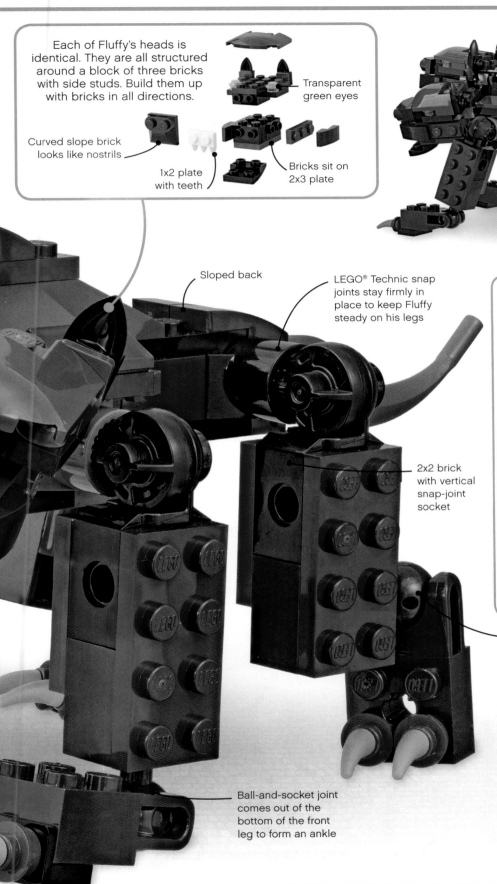

Sloped back

LEGO® Technic snap joints stay firmly in place to keep Fluffy steady on his legs

Sturdy legs

Fluffy's rear legs attach to a black 2x2 brick with snap connectors at either end. His wide-set front legs are attached separately. Each one has its own gray 2x2 brick with one connector. The joints are sandwiched between plates to lock them in place when the legs are moved.

2x2 brick with two connectors forms hips

2x2 brick with one connector

2x2 brick with vertical snap-joint socket

Ball-and-socket joint comes out of the side of the rear leg to mimic the way a real dog stands

Fluffy

Whether a creature has one head or three, four legs or one hundred, you can build it in the same way—one piece at a time. Fluffy is built around a simple core, to which legs, heads, and a tail are added. Use LEGO connectors to attach the limbs and make your creature easy to pose.

Ball-and-socket joint comes out of the bottom of the front leg to form an ankle

Devil's Snare

Harry, Hermione, and Ron escape from Fluffy through a trapdoor. A soft plant cushions their fall, but this is no ordinary plant. It's Devil's Snare: a deadly vine that attacks people. The more a victim wriggles and squirms, the tighter the plant grips.

JUST RELAX!

Vine trap

Harry got too close to the plant and now its tendrils have crept all around him! Fortunately, Hermione pays attention in Herbology. She tells Harry to relax and stop moving, and the plant will loosen its grip.

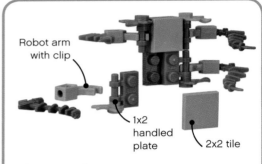

Robot arm with clip

1x2 handled plate

2x2 tile

Armed trap

Harry is caught by plant tendrils attached to robot arm pieces. These elements move on clip joints so they can be placed at different angles. Four should be enough to overpower a small minifigure such as Harry.

Mini Snares

Small shoots of Devil's Snare may look harmless, but they grow rapidly and can trap their victims in seconds. Use a range of different plant pieces to grow your own patch of Devil's Snare.

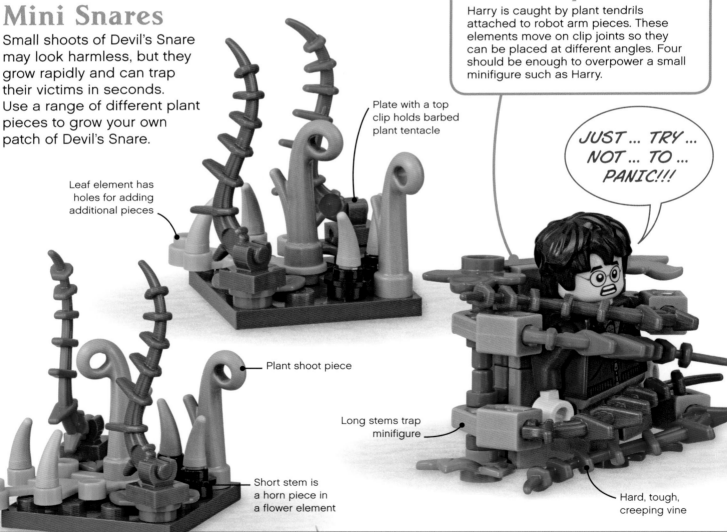

Leaf element has holes for adding additional pieces

Plate with a top clip holds barbed plant tentacle

Plant shoot piece

JUST ... TRY ... NOT ... TO ... PANIC!!!

Long stems trap minifigure

Short stem is a horn piece in a flower element

Hard, tough, creeping vine

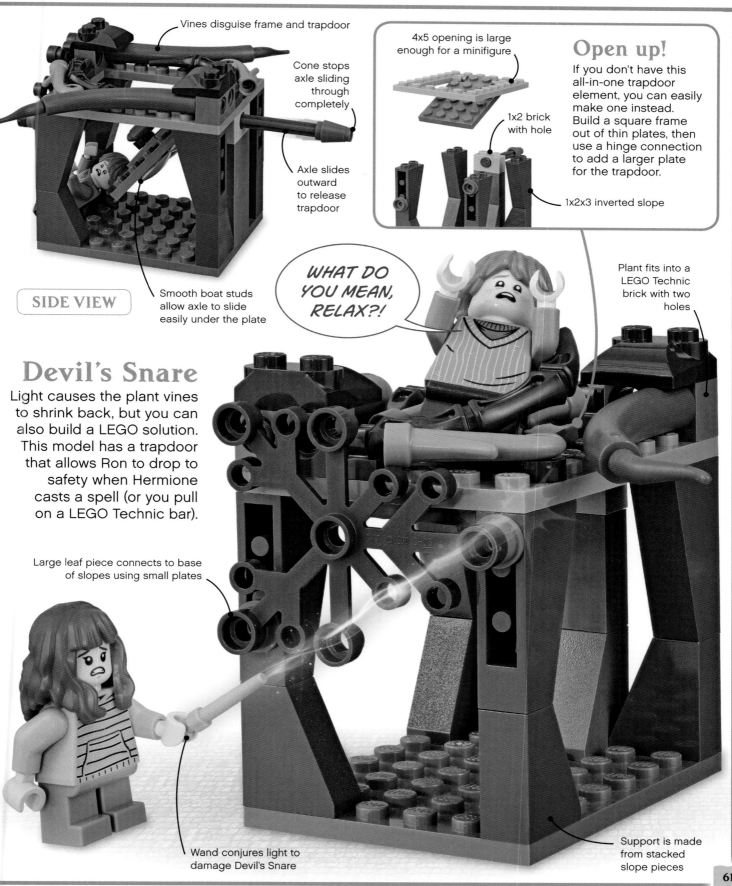

Vines disguise frame and trapdoor

Cone stops axle sliding through completely

Axle slides outward to release trapdoor

SIDE VIEW

Smooth boat studs allow axle to slide easily under the plate

4x5 opening is large enough for a minifigure

1x2 brick with hole

Open up!

If you don't have this all-in-one trapdoor element, you can easily make one instead. Build a square frame out of thin plates, then use a hinge connection to add a larger plate for the trapdoor.

1x2x3 inverted slope

WHAT DO YOU MEAN, RELAX?!

Plant fits into a LEGO Technic brick with two holes

Devil's Snare

Light causes the plant vines to shrink back, but you can also build a LEGO solution. This model has a trapdoor that allows Ron to drop to safety when Hermione casts a spell (or you pull on a LEGO Technic bar).

Large leaf piece connects to base of slopes using small plates

Wand conjures light to damage Devil's Snare

Support is made from stacked slope pieces

Wizard chess

Ron loves playing wizard chess, but his skills have never been tested on this level. Ron, Hermione, and Harry must play their way across the larger-than-life board in order to reach the Sorcerer's Stone. One wrong move and it's game over.

NOW THIS IS WIZARD CHESS!

Gray mane is made of slope pieces

KNIGHT TO H3!

Tail is a 1x4 slope clipped to a brick with handled bar

Silver horse armor

Chess pieces

You don't need to build a full chess set to give the idea of a game, just a few dark pieces and some light ones. These towering models have strong bases so they don't topple onto the minifigures!

Rocking horse

Ron has to grip tight to the Knight piece as it rears up on its back legs. Use a hinge brick to create the exciting angle. This angle also helps balance the model, as much of its weight is at the front.

1x2 slope sits under hinge brick

Angled bricks make an octagonal base

Chess board

Muggle chess is played on a distinctive black-and-white checkerboard, and wizard chess is no different! These 4x4 squares are a good scale for minifigure players, but you could use any size to conjure up your own scene.

Tan-colored base is two-plates deep

Use a whole plate for each square or fill the space using smaller plates

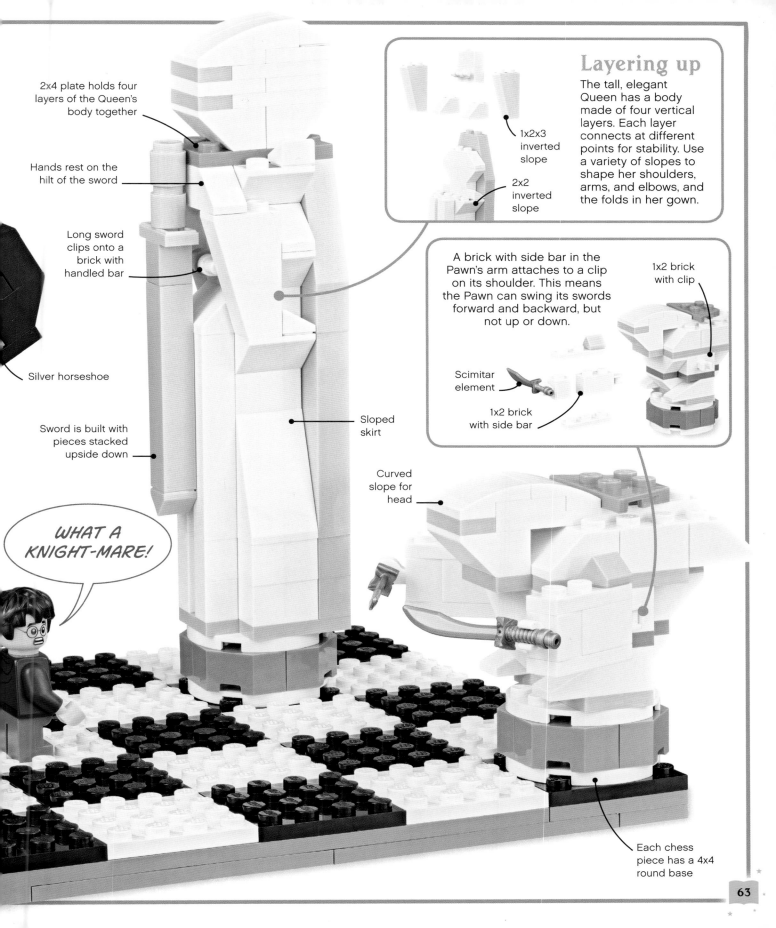

2x4 plate holds four layers of the Queen's body together

Hands rest on the hilt of the sword

Long sword clips onto a brick with handled bar

Silver horseshoe

Sword is built with pieces stacked upside down

WHAT A KNIGHT-MARE!

1x2x3 inverted slope

2x2 inverted slope

Layering up

The tall, elegant Queen has a body made of four vertical layers. Each layer connects at different points for stability. Use a variety of slopes to shape her shoulders, arms, and elbows, and the folds in her gown.

A brick with side bar in the Pawn's arm attaches to a clip on its shoulder. This means the Pawn can swing its swords forward and backward, but not up or down.

1x2 brick with clip

Scimitar element

1x2 brick with side bar

Sloped skirt

Curved slope for head

Each chess piece has a 4x4 round base

2-in-1 model

When Harry arrives for his first year at Hogwarts, he takes part in a special Sorting Ceremony. The enchanted Sorting Hat is placed on Harry's head and it decides which of the four Hogwarts houses he belongs in … GRYFFINDOR! Gryffindors are brave and determined witches and wizards.

Pointed spires and turrets are common at Hogwarts

Burning torches

Flickering candle

PLEASE—NOT SLYTHERIN!

Magical fireplace

The Sorting Hat spinner can be transformed into a magical fireplace. Harry stands on one side of the fireplace, with flames on the other. A quick spin and he can move magically between rooms without being seen!

A tile shows which house the fireplace belongs to

Chest contains magic spell book

Minifigure platform

Ancient stone walls

Spin the turntable to pick a house

Spinner instructions

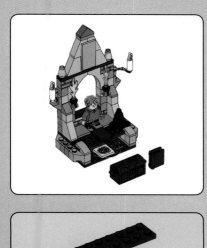

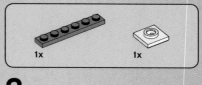
3

1

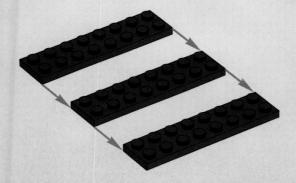

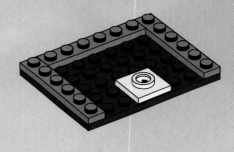

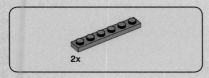
2

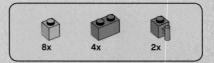
4

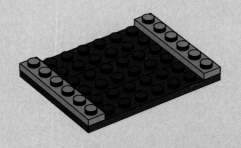

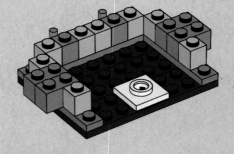

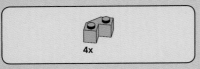

4x

5

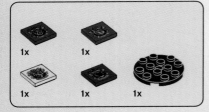

1x   1x

1x   1x   1x

6

1   2

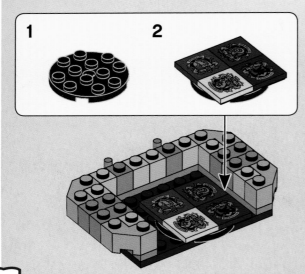

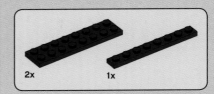

2x   1x

7

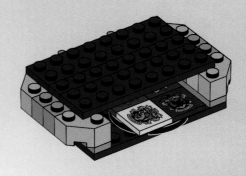

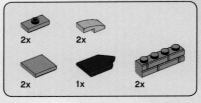

2x   2x

2x   1x   2x

8

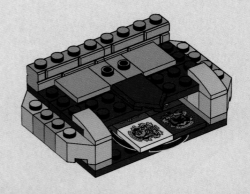

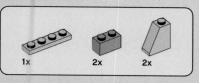

9

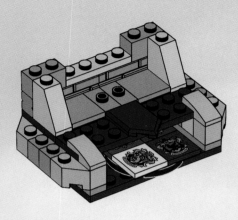

10

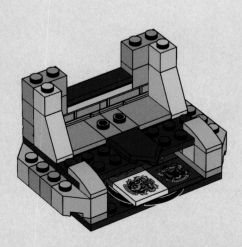

11

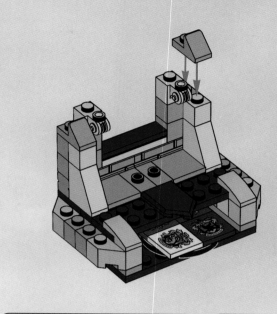

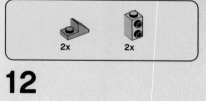

12

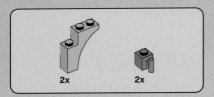

2x   2x

13

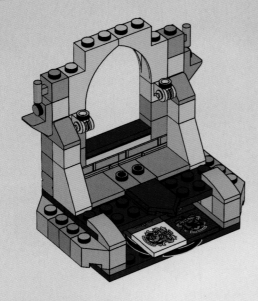

1x

15

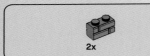

2x

14

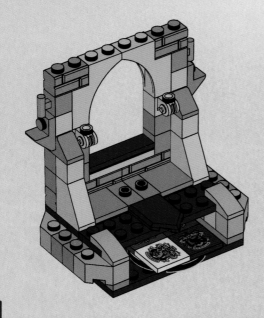

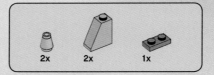

2x   2x   1x

16

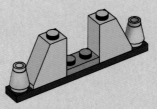

17

2x

18

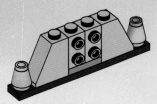

2x

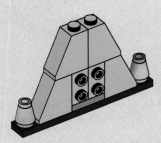

19

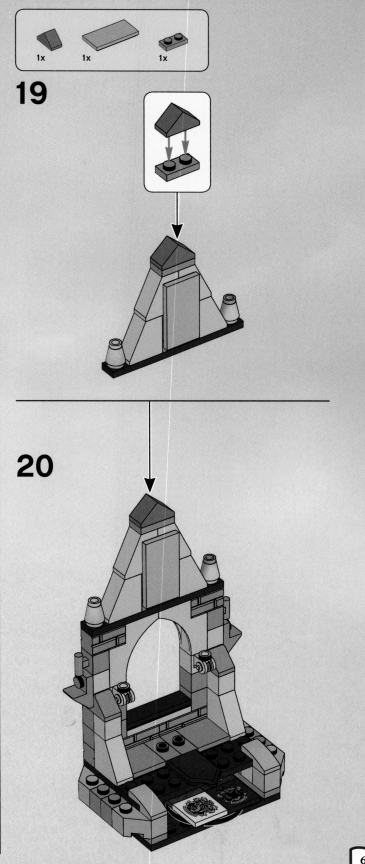

1x 1x 1x

20

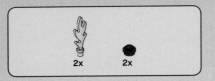

2x   2x

2x   2x   2x

2x

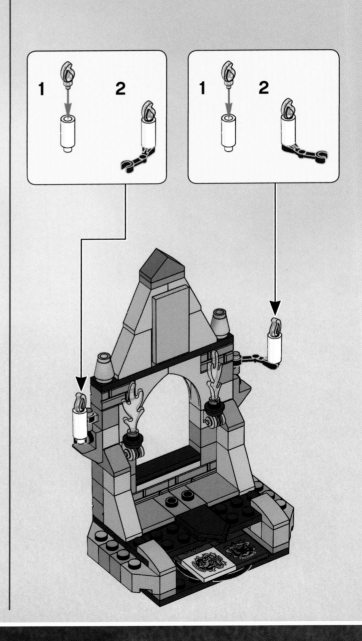

1   2   1   2

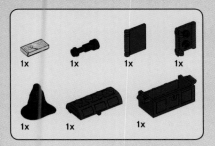

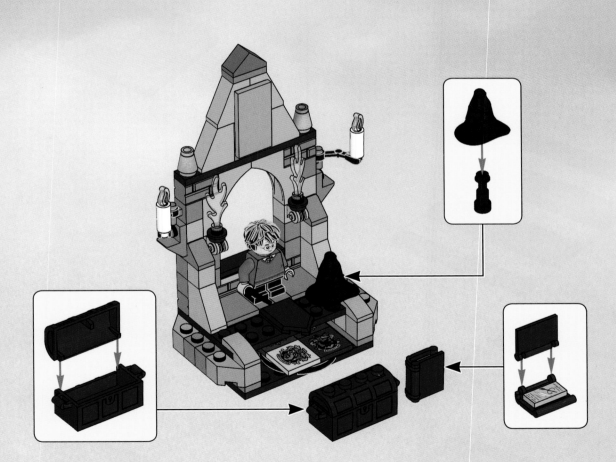

Fireplace instructions

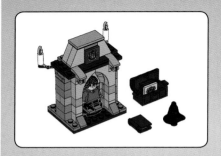

2x   2x

1

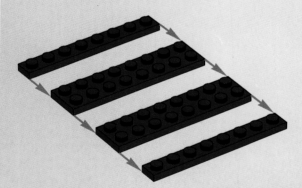

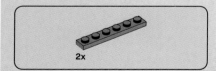

2x

2

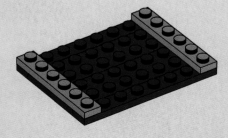

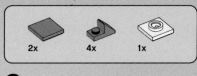

2x   4x   1x

3

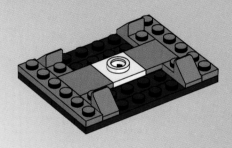

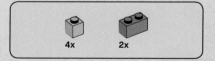

4x   2x

4

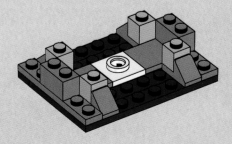

1x   1x   2x   2x

5

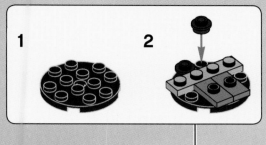

1   **2**

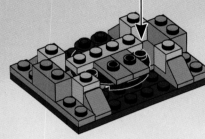

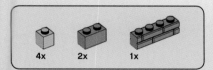

4x   2x   1x

6

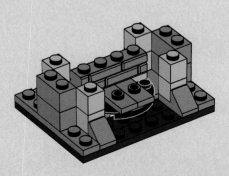

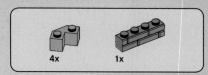

4x   1x

7

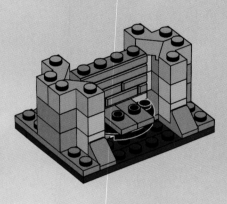

2x   2x   2x   2x

8

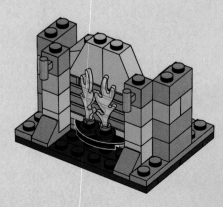

9

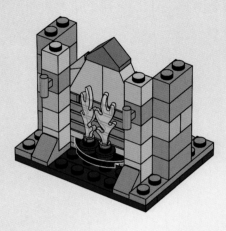

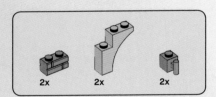

10

11

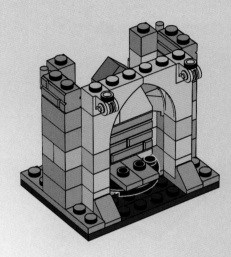

12

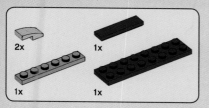

2x
1x
1x
1x

13

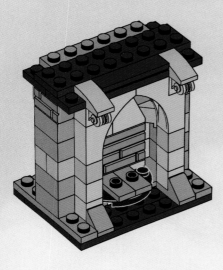

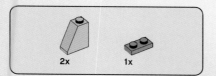

2x
1x

14

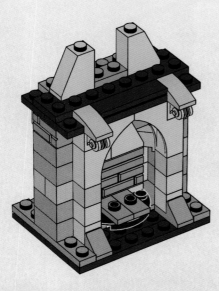

4x

15

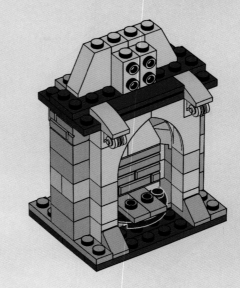

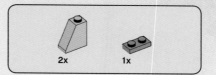

2x
1x

16

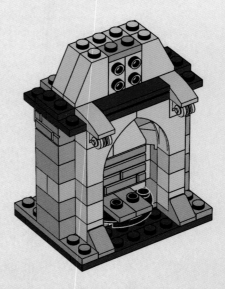

1x   1x

17

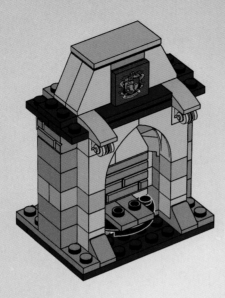

2x   1x

18

2x   2x   2x

19

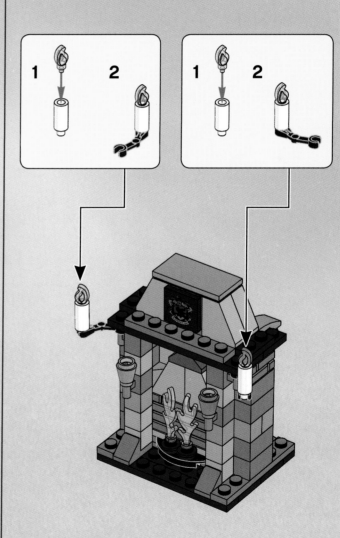

1   2   1   2

1x 1x 1x

20

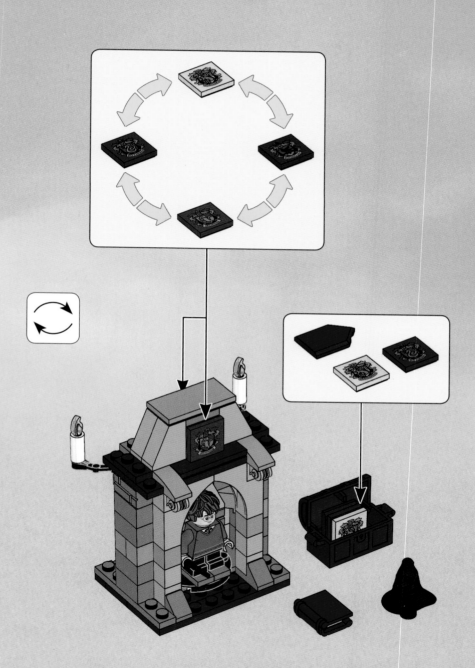

Editor Beth Davies
Designer Sam Bartlett
Senior Pre-Production Producer Jennifer Murray
Senior Producer Louise Daly
Managing Editor Paula Regan
Managing Art Editor Jo Connor
Publisher Julie Ferris
Art Director Lisa Lanzarini
Publishing Director Simon Beecroft

Written by Elizabeth Dowsett
Inspirational models built by Marcos Bessa,
James Stephenson, Luis Castañeda,
Raphaël Pretesacque, Woon Tze Chee,
Mark Stafford, and Joel Baker.
Photography by Gary Ombler

Dorling Kindersley would like also like to thank
Randi K. Sørensen, Heidi K. Jensen, Paul Hansford, Martin
Leighton Lindhard, and Helene Desprets at the LEGO Group.
Thanks also to Lisa Sodeau and James McKeag for design
assistance, Vicky Armstrong and Megan Douglass for editorial
assistance, and Mark Bollans for the use of his minifigure.

First American Edition, 2019
Published in the United States by DK Publishing
1450 Broadway, Suite 801, New York, NY 10018

Copyright © 2019 Dorling Kindersley Limited
DK, a Division of Penguin Random House LLC
19 20 21 22 23 10 9 8 7 6 5 4 3 2 1
001–312822–July/19

A catalog record for this book
is available from the Library of Congress.

ISBN 978-1-4654-8361-4

DK books are available at special discounts when purchased
in bulk for sales promotions, premiums, fund-raising, or
educational use. For details, contact: DK Publishing Special
Markets, 1450 Broadway, Suite 801, New York, NY 10018
SpecialSales@dk.com

Printed in China

www.LEGO.com
www.dk.com

A WORLD OF IDEAS:
SEE ALL THERE IS TO KNOW